This brrrilliant
book belongs to:

....

To Polly
K.G.

For Xander, the biggest dino fan
N.E.

HODDER CHILDREN'S BOOKS
First published in Great Britain in 2022
by Hodder and Stoughton

10 9 8 7 6 5 4 3 2 1

Text © Kes Gray, 2022
Illustrations © Nick East, 2022

A CIP catalogue record for this book is available
from the British Library.

HB ISBN 978 1 44493 435 9
PB ISBN 978 1 44493 436 6

Printed and bound in China

MIX
Paper from
responsible sources
FSC® C104740
FSC
www.fsc.org

HODDER CHILDREN'S BOOKS
An imprint of Hachette Children's Group
Part of Hodder and Stoughton
Carmelite House, 50 Victoria Embankment,
London EC4Y 0DZ

An Hachette UK Company
www.hachette.co.uk
www.hachettechildrens.co.uk

BRRR!

WHERE DID THE DINOSAURS REALLY GO?

KES GRAY

NICK EAST

HODDER

The Ice Age was coming...

the temperatures were dropping and all the dinosaurs were getting very worried.

"How cold is it going to get?" asked the brontosauruses.

"Freezing cold," said the stegosauruses.

"Minus a million BC*," said the triceratopses.

*Before Centigrade

"Too cold for sabre-toothed tigers," shuddered the sabre-toothed tigers. "Even too cold for woolly mammoths!"

"What are we going to do?" shivered the pterodactyls.

"We need to knit some jumpers," said the brontosauruses, "and we need to knit them fast."

All the dinosaurs had a go at knitting jumpers, but it was hopeless. The brontosauruses couldn't pick up the knitting needles, the stegosauruses kept treading on the knitting patterns and the pterodactyls kept getting tangled up in the wool.

"It's no good," sighed the brontosauruses, "dinosaurs just aren't designed to knit jumpers!"

"T-Rexes are," said Silvisaurus.
"Look how short their arms
are. They'd be perfect for
knitting jumpers!"

All the dinosaurs
looked at the T-Rexes
and gulped.

"We can't ask the T-Rexes to knit jumpers," said the stegosaruses. "Look how scary they are."

"We're not asking them. You go and ask them," said the brontosauruses.

"We're not asking them. You go and ask them," said the sabre-toothed tigers.

"We're not asking them. You go and ask them," said the woolly mammoths.

"What if they chase us? What if they catch us? What if they eat us?!" said the oviraptors.

"I'll go and ask them," sighed Silvisaurus . . .

"JUMPERS!" roared the T-Rexes. "YOU WANT US TO KNIT JUMPERS?! WE'RE THE TOUGHEST, MEANEST, WELL-HARDEST DINOSAURS ON THE PLANET! WE'RE NOT ABOUT TO KNIT JUMPERS!"

BOOM BOOM

BOOM
BOOM

GULP

"But you're perfectly designed to knit jumpers," explained Silvisaurus. "You have the height to knit BIG and your arms are, well . . . just the right length!"

"OUR ARMS MIGHT BE THE RIGHT LENGTH BUT THEY ARE NOT, REPEAT **NOT**, HERE TO KNIT JUMPERS!" roared the T-Rexes. "**OUR ARMS ARE HERE TO GO . . .**

"What did the T-Rexes say?"
asked the dinosaurs when
Silvisaurus returned.

"Oh dear," shivered the dinosaurs as the first snowflakes began to fall . . .

And fall, and fall, and fall.

"**BRRRRRRRRR**," shivered the stegosauruses. After **twenty** days of snowfall, their teeth were beginning to chatter.

"**BRRRRRRRRRR**," shivered the diplodocuses.

After **fifty** days of snowfall,
their noses were turning blue.

"BRRRRRRRRRRRRRRRRRRRRRRRRRRRRRRRRRRRRRRR,"
shivered the brontosauruses.
After **eighty** days of snowfall,
they couldn't feel their toes or
the tips of their tails.

By the **hundredth** day, even the T-Rexes were shivering.

"**ALL RIGHT!**" they sighed. "We'll knit some jumpers!"

Silvisaurus was right – the T-Rexes were brilliant at knitting jumpers.
In fact, they were so good, they even knitted Christmas ones!

And **then** they extended their Ice Age range to bobble hats, mittens and scarves!

CLAP CLAP HOORAY

The colder the Ice Age became, the warmer the dinosaurs wrapped up.

But every day, the Ice Age temperatures fell even further.

"You couldn't knit us some onesies, could you?" asked the dinosaurs.

"We'll give it a go," said the T-Rexes.

The T-Rexes' onesies were **amazing**.

But still the Ice Age temperatures continued to fall . . .

"**BRRRRRRRRRRRRRRR,**" brrred the dinosaurs.
"You couldn't knit us some houses, could you?"

It was a big ask, but the T-Rexes were BIG on knitting needles too.

CLINK   CLINK

All the dinosaurs moved into their new **knitted** houses
and curled up on their new knitted sofas.

But still the Ice Age temperatures continued to fall . . .

and fall, and fall,

and fall.

"BBBBBrrrrrrrrrrrrrrrrrrrrRrr,"

shivered the dinosaurs. "We think you might have to knit us a new planet — somewhere high above the Earth that's lovely and woolly and warm."

CLICK CLICK

CLICKERTY CLICK

The T-Rexes loved a **BIG**, **BIG** challenge and they threw themselves at the task.
They **even** knitted huge rockets that could carry all the dinosaurs into space.

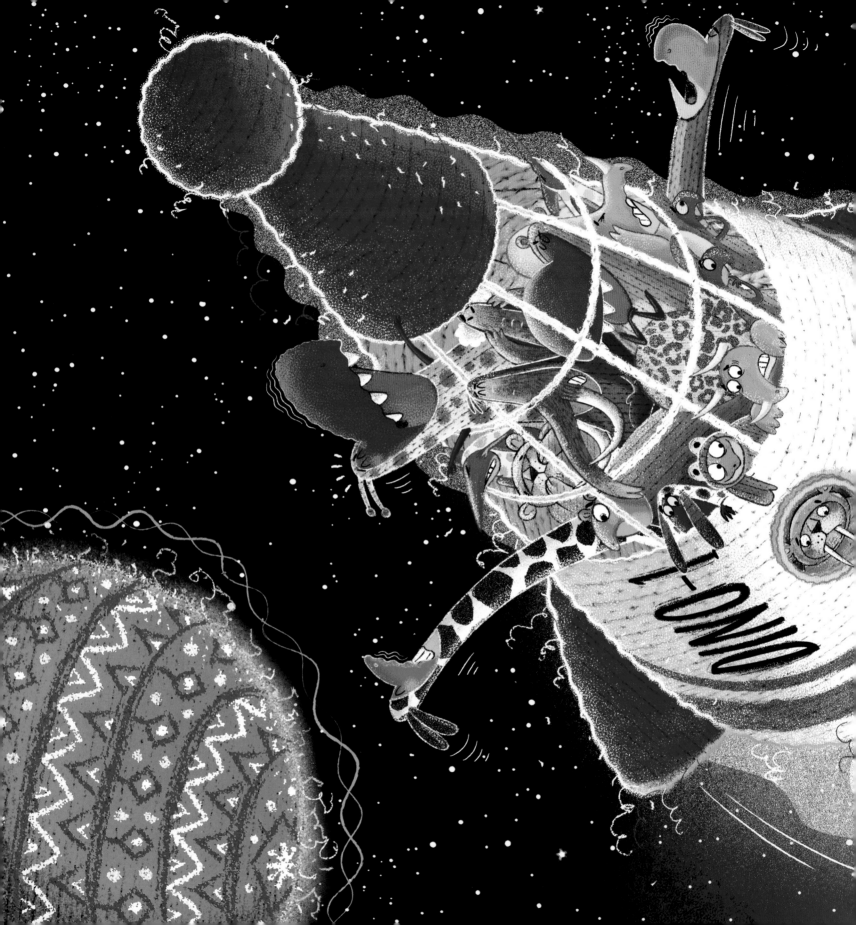

"ALL ABOARD!" they roared.

"Planet Pla-knit, here we come!"

The dinosaurs took off in their woollen rocket
and waved goodbye to planet Earth.

"WAIT!" shouted the T-Rexes.

"If we vanish from the face of the Earth in our rocket,
you don't think people will one day think that
dinosaurs have died out do you?"

"You're right," said Silvisaurus, "how will they know that we left planet Earth to start a much warmer and woollier life on planet Pla-knit?"

"**How about we send them a knitted postcard?**" said the brontosauruses.